LITTLE WOLF

Terror of the Shivery Sea

First American edition published in 2004
by Carolrhoda Books, Inc.
published by arrangement with
HarperCollins Publishers Ltd., London, England

Text copyright © 2004 by Ian Whybrow
Illustrations copyright © 2004 by Tony Ross

Carolrhoda Books, Inc.
A division of Lerner Publishing Group
241 First Avenue North
Minneapolis, MN 55401 U.S.A.

Website address: www.carolrhodabooks.com

Library of Congress Cataloging-in-Publication Data

Whybrow, Ian.
Little Wolf, terror of the Shivery Sea / by Ian Whybrow ; illustrated by
Tony Ross.—1st American ed.
p. cm.
Summary: In a series of letters to his parents, Little Wolf tells of
setting sail to find the lost treasure of his legendary ancestor, Blackfur
the Pirate.
ISBN: 1–57505–629–1 (lib. bdg. : alk. paper)
[1. Pirates—Fiction. 2. Wolves—Fiction. 3. Letters—Fiction.]
I. Ross, Tony, ill. II. Title.
PZ7.W6225Lhe 2004
[Fic]—dc22   2003026083

Manufactured in the United States of America
1 2 3 4 5 6 – BP – 09 08 07 06 05 04

LITTLE
Terror of the Shivery Sea
WOLF

IAN WHYBROW ILLUSTRATED BY TONY ROSS

Carolrhoda Books, Inc./ Minneapolis

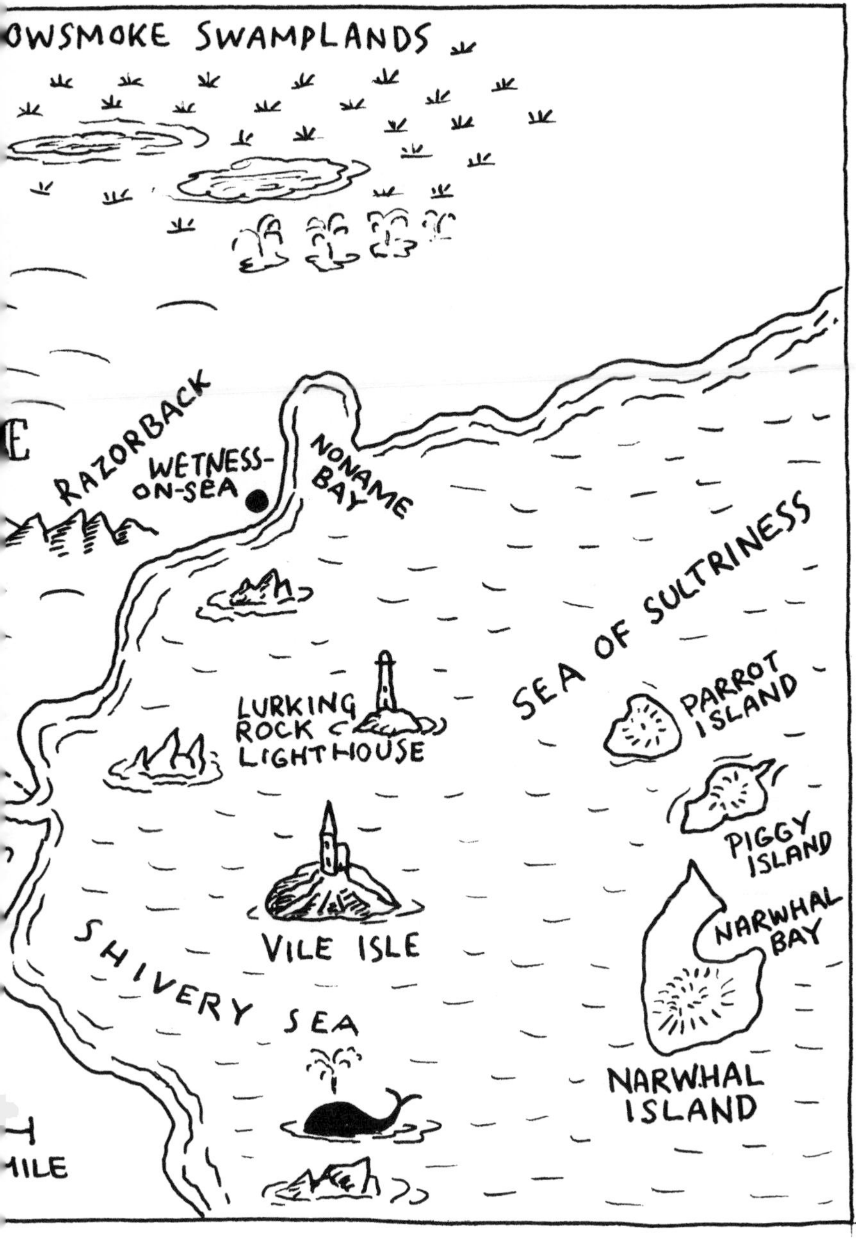

OWSMOKE SWAMPLANDS

RAZORBACK
WETNESS-ON-SEA
NONAME BAY

SEA OF SULTRINESS

PARROT ISLAND

LURKING ROCK LIGHTHOUSE

PIGGY ISLAND

VILE ISLE

NARWHAL BAY

SHIVERY SEA

NARWHAL ISLAND

MILE

For my faithful readers, Marcus and Michael Powell, and for their granddad, Tom, who looks after the lot of us.

My Desk

Dear Mom and Dad,

Please, please, PLEEEEEZ take Smells back to Murkshire to stay with you at the den. Go on, just for a short while, like ten years maybe, hint, hint. You know he is your darling baby pet. Plus you are a lot fiercer than me, so you can stop him from messing up your stuff.

Yeller wants me do trick practiss with him. Tricks are 1 of my favorite things. I love them, kiss, kiss. BUT (big but) Smells keeps messing us up. Like if you are trying to have a private ~~conservash~~ ~~condensayshun~~ chat about fake bat poo or itchy powder, Smells keeps butting in hummingly.

Also, he pulls down his sailor suit bottoms, saying, "Look at my underpants. They have Stooffer the Steam Engine on them, har, har!" Just because he is jealous of my underpants saying Wiggly World, I bet.

So cubbish.

I wish, wish, **wishhhh** you would take him back, because now he has got the habit of going **Blah Blah** in a loud way until you play Doctor Monster with him. He makes you pretend to be ill in bed so he can do harsh operations on you that really hurt.

You have him for a bit. He is your cub. I am only his big bro, so not fair, eh?

Yours snuggluply,

L. Wolf, son numero un (French)

Uncle Bigbad's **OLD PLACE,**
Frettnin Forest, Beastshire

Kitchen Table

Dear Mom and Dad,

You have not replied to my letter about taking back Smells. I know you have been having a nice long winter hibernate. Maybe it is best to say my friends' names for you in an xplainy way. (Just in case your branes are shut down still, OK?)

Now (xplainy voice) my best friend and cuz is Yeller Wolf. He has got loads of BIG IDEAS and SHOUTS a lot.

My next best friends are Normus Bear
(whopping mussuls)

and Stubbs Crow (clever beak,
says "ARK!" a lot).

These are some
adventures we have
done before, OK?

turn over

* Daring Deeds at Adventure Academy.

* Haunting at Haunted Hall with dead Uncle Bigbad as our best ghost. (He died of eating 2 many bakebeans 2 fast and went bang, remember?)

* Being Frettnin Forest Detective Agency. That was good.

* Camping out, tracking, etc., with me as Pack Leader.

Now we are trying to think up another adventure to have, but Smells is spoiling it for us. NOT FAIR.

Yours remindingly,

L. Wolf, son

Down the Coalhole

Dear Mud and Dam,

Thank you for your sharp note saying stop
reminding people. Also you do not like me
saying about your branes being shut down, so I
must lock myself in the coalhole. OK, but
serves you right if this writing is crooked
(dark in here).

About saying "Yes?" and "Hmmm?" and all that.
You say that is a big nerve, talking to you in an
xplainy way, because you are big parents, not
small weaky fluffballs. So, now I must suck a bar
of soap, OR ELSE. Plus I must *pack up whining*
and saying *not fair.*

13

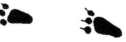 

OK, I will count myself lucky being able to spend time with my baby bro, but can you check your clock to see how long that time is? I think it has gotten stuck.

Yours punishedly,

Little Filthy (coal dust)

P.S. I have not done the soapsucking part yet. Sorry, but I cannot do my best at writing plus spitting out bubbles at the same time.

P.P.S. I am doing it now, spit, spit, bluck.

Drawer Number 3 (aah cozy),
Chester Drawers, My Room

Dear Mom and Dad,

Shame about Dad catching a touch of the
mange and being all germy. You say Smellybreff
cannot come near Dad for ages, because he
might catch it. His fur will be itchy and drop off
in rug-size lumps, ooo-er.

Yes, I understand Dad is being noble in a wolfly way (if he is not telling a whopping FAT FIB, hint, hint). By the way, is the mange like the dessert

blancmange? Because you never get fur on that either. Funny, eh? Only if you leave it out of the fridge for a week.

Yours askingly,

Son Wun

Dear M and D,

You know when I was down the coalhole sucking soap for getting on your nerves? Well, I found a dusty old pic thrown out by Uncle Bigbad, a big 1 with a fancy frame.

I thought I'd give it a soapy lick, see who is under the dust. Then I found out. It is a fearsome old wolf with beard, scar, etc., all covered in guns and daggers! He has a funny hat on with a bones badge made out of jewels, all sparkly like his earring. He has got a cruel, teasy look on his face, and he is sitting on a big, strong, old chest. In his paw, he is holding a long, twisty stick. It looks like rock candy, only made of elephant tusks, maybe.

I gave the sign underneath a good shine with my fur so you can see some words. They are:

Blackfur the Backbiter.

I wonder who that Blackfur was. I bet he was an olden-day park keeper that was all snarly and snappish, yes?

Yours surmisingly,

Detective Inspectacles Wolf
(get it?)

P.S. Clue: it is me wearing spectacles, really.

Uncle Bigbad's **OLD PLACE**,
Frettnin Forest, Beastshire

Sofa, Sitting Room

Dear Mom and Dad,

Surmisingly is not a fake word. It is a real 1, honest. I found it in a detecting book. So, I thought, give it a short tryout in your next letter.

Sorry it made Dad go "Grrrr," but maybe that was just his normal temper. Or the mange. Or sitting on a hedgehog.

Thank you for your answer to the pic I found down the coalhole. I have hung it in the hall now because you say it is a family portrait of our great wolfly ancestor Blackfur the Rat Pie, Terror of All the Sea.

No wonder Uncle Bigbad got jealous and threw it away. Uncle did not want anywun to know there was a bigger Terror than him, I bet!

1 small thing I still do not get is how can a rat pie be a Terror of anything? I love rat pies (yum, yum, not scary 1 bit).

Yours puzzledly,

Little

Uncle Bigbad's **OLD PLACE**,
Frettnin Forest, Beastshire

Tree Stump, the Garden

Dear Mom and Dad,

Still no news from you about rat pies, boo, shame.

I am writing this in pencil, but do not sing:

Har, Har bubbacub, you are just a blubbercub.

You know I hate writing in pencil, but it is all Smells's fault. Today is my worst day this week, because of Smells meeting a raccoon with a mask on in Frettnin Forest. After that he got jealous, saying he wanted to have a mask 2 and be Mister Burgle-Arrr the Robber.

I 'spect you will say, "Oh, well done, Smellybreff, my fine baby cub. Now you are following in Daddy's pawprints." But listen, Yeller and me said well done to him 2! We said, "Fine, well done, you *can* be a burgle-arrr, Smells. But only if you stick to robbing ants, piggies, etc., OK?"

Sad to say, he did not listen. He went and robbed all my furniture and hid it. So now no bed to sleep on, no chester drawers, etc. And Smells drinks all my ink just for spitefulness. Floors are my least favorite thing for sleeping on. It made me get up stiffly in the morning time needing a warm-up trot outside. Off I went joggingly, then guess what? A **BIG** moose came rushing! He tried to stop me with his horns—a **BIG** moose! All because of Smells robbing his grass from him!

Yours moaningly,

Little

P.S. Good thing Normus came along and gave that moose a hard thump.

My Bed (again, hmmm, snuggly),
My Room

Dear Mom and Dad,

Today I feel a lot more cheery because of finding a big haystack by Beech Grove. Only, it was not a haystack really. It was my furniture buried in moose grass by Smells.

Also, a big **Arrrr00000,** to Smells for stopping bugging me (mostly). That is because he has gone all soppy over Normus for having big mussuls and bashing that moose. (By the way, it was quite tasty. Lipsmack, lipsmack.)

23

Now Smells is busy outside playing Jack and the Cabbagestalk with Normus. Smells lets both of them be the giant-bashers, so Normus likes it 2. Sometimes they creep up behind people, going bonk.

I was that person 1 time, so I said a loud *Ouch!* Then Smells went and cuddled Normus's leg, saying to me, "Be quiet, Little. I only like Normus now!"

Funny, I did not know he liked me before. Oh well. Never mind, as long as he leaves me alone. Now I can have a quiet read and maybe find a nice new adventure to have.

By the way, I got your short card saying, **WAKE UP!!!!** Plus saying, "Your faymus ancestor Blackfur was a Pie Rat not a Rat Pie. He was sitting on a chest full of treasure, so get out of bed and go find it NOW!"

Sorry, I still do not get it. What does that mean, Pie Rat?

Yours headscratchingly,

Little Dimp

Dear Mom and Dad,

Oh, I get it now. Blackfur was a Pie Rat spelled PIRATE! I asked Stubbs, and he said, "ARK!" meaning look it up in the en*cark*lopedia. So we did. Sad to say, I only read a short part. Just then, Smells came by playing Jack and the Cabbagestalk. He chopped up the page I was reading with his chopper. Then he ate it, saying,

"Bee By Bo Bum,
I like paper, yum, yum, yum."

Not funny.

Normus said, "Hey, be fair Smells— no eating pages. Save that for big giants." Smells did not like Normus telling him off, so he chopped up his trout net saying, "Be quiet, Normus. I only like Yeller now!"

I said (wise voice), "There, I told you he was only a short friend, Normus."
That is Y Normus has gone off to sulk.
I can hear him outside hitting trees—*bonk*, e e - a r r r, **crash**.

I'm lucky Yeller still wants to be my pal.

Yours shameshamely,

Little Cheesedoff

Dear Mom and Dad,

Soon, I will have no friends left. It is all your fault because of making me look after your cruel baby. Also, how can I find Blackfur's treasure when I have to keep cub-sitting my baby bro?

Did I say about Smells wanting to be Mister Tricker? What about him having a big crush on Yeller for showing him lots of good tricks? Trouble is, Smells only likes trying the tricks out on me. Here's two of them:

The Fridge Trick

Smells comes running into the kitchen, saying, "Hello, Little. Is your fridge running? Good, now it is running out the window." Then he pushes it out, saying, "Har, har, tricked you!"

Another Wun:

This morning, Smells swallowed a bunch
of my Lego pieces. Then he pressed his tummy
button and threw them all up, saying, "Look,
me a toaster. Pop, pop!"

That was a funny wun,
so I fell over laughing.
But guess what?
He said, "Shut up,
Sillyfur. I only like
Yeller." So harsh.

Yours jealously,

Little

P.S. I am 2 upset to xplain now, so more
tomorrow.

Inside My Closet (having a dark curl-up),
My Room

Dear Mom and Dad,

Here are Yeller's last words that he said to me doorslammingly. (In a note—he rolled them up, then skwashed them through my keyhole.)

LISTEN LICKLE, I AM ALL FED UP. I TRIED BEIN NICE TO SMELLS, HIM BEIN ONLY A KID, BUT NOW HE AS GON 2 FAR. HE KEPT ON PESTERIN ME TO TEACH HIM MORE AND MORE TRICKS. SO IN THE END, I THOUGHT, I KNOW, I WILL TRY TO DOUBLE-TRICK HIM. I SAID, "SMELLS, YOU ARE SUCH A GOOD TRICKER, YOU MUST NEVER, NEVER, NEVER PLAY MISTER TIDYUP, OK?" THAT MADE HIM GET ALL CRAFTY-LOOKIN.

THEN OFF HE WENT
RUSHIN AND DID A
TiDYUP OF HIS ROOM. SO
I SAID, "WELL DONE, ME"
TO MYSELF, bUT THEN HE
WENT AND PULLED A
bUNCH OF FEATHERS OUT
OF STUBBS'S TAIL FOR A
DUSTER. tHEY WERE THE
WUNS STUBBS WAS SAVIN
SPECIAL FOR LOOPIN THE
LOOP, SO HE GAVE ME A
HARSH PECK! ALL YOUR
FAULT FOR HAVIN SMELLS
AS A BAbY BRO. I AM
NOT STAYIN HERE 1 SINGLE
SHORT SEC LONGER, SO
TUFF, BANG, DOORSLAM!

And now Stubbs just hid up the chimney,
saying, "ARK!" meaning he will never darken
my doorknob again.

Yours leftalonely,

L., etc. (2 upset to write all of
my name down, so there)

Dear Mom and Dad,

I am all sad without Yeller and Normus here, but good news about Stubbs. He did not like me going snifful in my hanky. Out of the chimney hole he popped with a nice present (a beakful of crawlycreeps for a snack). Then off he went flappingly down the shop. He fetched me a copy of *Wolf Weekly*, so he and me could have a nice newsy read together.

Guess what we read in the paper? There is ANOTHER Terror of the Shivery Sea. They say he is even more of a Terror than our ancestor Blackfur the Backbiter. This 1 is called Captain Froshus. Ooo-er!

Stubbs has cut this story out for you with his clever beak. Do you like it? It has got some fine ~~dizgiz deskies~~ (cannot spell it) dressing up in it.

Your own cub reporter (get it?),

Little Wolf

Terror on the Shivery Sea

Once again, the mysterious Captain Froshus, Master of *The Seafox*, is gaining a reputation as the most ruthless and terrifying pirate ever to sail the Shivery Sea.

cunning disguise

It is said that Captain Froshus has gathered a harsh crew that includes polecats, weasles, and vicious wild boars to do his dirty work. They specialize in cunning disguise. So for the moment, the true identity of the captain and crew remain cloaked in secrecy.

witness speaks

Meanwhile, yesterday, three miles off No-name Bay, *The Seafox* captured two fishing boats: *The Kipper* and *The Slippery Eel*. Ricky Walrus, mate of *The Kipper*, spoke to our reporter once he was safely aboard the Swamplands lifeboat.

"We had no chance!" he said. "We was just doing a bit of trawling, when we saw this schooner sailing up astern. The boat must have been lurking up a creek somewhere. We didn't take much notice, because her crew was no more than a bunch of girlies wearing flowery dresses. Then snip my flipper if her crew didn't hoist the Snarl and Wishbones and shoot off our rudder with a cannonball! Then she come right alongside, and after that it was Swish, Swush, Sploosh until I wound up in the drink, minus me wallet and me watch!"

victim tells all

Just before going to press, *Wolf Weekly* has learned from one of the victims of *The Slippery Eel*, Able Sealion "Honks" Greymuzzle, that for several hours he was questioned at pistol-point by Captain Froshus himself. The captain kept asking what he knew about the hidden treasure of the legendary pirate, Blackfur the Backbiter. Recovering last night in a warm cabin in River Riggly, the stunned victim told our reporter that he knew nothing about any hidden treasure or any pirate called Blackfur the Backbiter. Asked to describe Captain Froshus, Able Sealion Greymuzzle said that he couldn't see Froshus's face because he was wearing a mask. However, *Wolf Weekly* was told that Froshus spoke very softly, had big staring eyes, and smelled strongly of pepper.

warning!

Be warned, readers! No vessel, brute beast, or seaside home is safe from the heartless ways of these wicked plunderers. And the shaming fact is that among the whole shocking crew, there is not one single wolf!

Editorial: p. 15: **Running Out of Huff?** Modern wolves slip down the ranks of the Most Wicked List

Dear Em and Dee,

Thank you for your
very fast package saying:

"Hurry up and show Smells a good example.
Forget doing reading and Run Away to Sea
THIS MINUTE!!!"

You say that I MUST FIND Blackfur's lost
treasure for you before Captain Froshus gets his
paws on it. But if Captain Froshus finds it 1st, it is
up to me to get it from him, so that I keep up our
fearsome family name of Wolf.

Yes, I got the tape of you singing. You say it is
an old pack song, s'posed to be from Blackfur's
time. It goes:

> *Seek my treasure in the bay,*
> *Where the unicorn doth play!*
> *Those who seek without a map,*
> *Mind the teeth that snarl and snap!*
> *Lucky those who most do itch,*
> *Scratch and lo, ye shall be rich!*

Har, har, good joke. Just listen to the funny
words. Also, even bubbercubs know there is no
such thing as unicorns, they are just a ~~lejunds~~
l~~e~~dg~~e~~nd story. Now Smells has
burgled the tape from me so he
can play it on his Walkwolf and
do dancing.

chinkle
plink
plink

Yes, I do understand the most
important part of your message. The
part about how all that gold and jewels, etc.,
belong to you really, because you are the nearest
ancestors to Blackfur in the Wolf family, yes? That
xplains the foamy photo of himself that Dad sent.
I thought, funny, I did not know Dad liked
shaving. But no, he was not shaving. He was just
foaming at the mouth from being greedy.

You say, addingly,
a Mind You like
this, "Mind you,
it is a bit too
dangerous for our
darling baby pet
Smellybreff to go
Running Away
to Sea, because

he might get killed or worse." I must seek my sulky friends swiftly and pass on this message from you. It is "Hey, Yeller, Normus, and Stubbs, stop being hopeless and make yourself useful. Grrrrr, you stay put, then you can be guards for our Smellybreff."

OK, I will try my hardest to make up with them, but I think Yeller and Normus have gone away (all because of youknowwho).

Yours seekingly,

The Panter

A Needly Glade, Piney Part,
Frettnin Forest

Dear Mom and Dad,

It is hard work keeping up
our fearsome name of Wolf, so
now I am having a sit-down
on a short heap of pine
needles. My friends must
be having a curl-up
down a deep hole or in
a cave somewhere. I
have looked and looked
and still no luck.

Will you send me EVERYTHING you know
about Blackfur and pirate ways? Smells ate the
pirate page out of the encyclopedia. Remember?
It's no good for me to chase after Blackfur's
treasure cluelessly. Maybe you have got a treasure
map tucked up a drawer somewhere, hmmm?

Your hunting son,

Little Beagle

Uncle Bigbad's **OLD PLACE**,
Frettnin Forest, Beastshire

Indoors (again, by stained glass window with magnifying glass), Big Hall

Dear Mom,

No ~~map~~ from you, boo shame, never mind. But Mom, can you do the writing next time? Dad's ~~skrigs~~ ~~skrorl~~ scribble joined-up letters are a bit 2 rushing for me. (Just because he cannot wait to have a gloat over *that* lost treasure, I bet.)

I have tried reading Dad's tips about Blackfur and pirate ways, but it is hard for small eyes. I think I get the 1st part. It says Dad does not know much about Blackfur, so stop asking. Then the next part goes something like, "They add windy botts." Does Dad mean pirates used the strong wind to sail their *boats*? I hope so. If not, hold your noses. Phew.

Also:

- What is, "Ho yoyo and a bobble of rug?"
- What does he mean by "welking the plonk?"
- Dad says (I think), "Pirates like capturing loads of booties." Why? Have they got lots of babies with chilly feet?
- Is he sure about "snotted hankies around their heads?" (Errrr, rude habits!)
- Dad, do you mean pirates *do* big pants or they *wear* big pants?
- Also how can you chop off people's heads with "cute lass?"

Yours onlyaskingly,

Little

Boot Room, Next to the Pantry

Dear Dad,

Sorry. I forgot, Dad, wolves are not s'posed to write proply. Also they do not like to keep on saying answers. So tuff luck me, I must find out about Blackfur and pirate ways bymyselfly. Plus, I must get out on the seawater and find Blackfur's treasure AT WUNCE before the shocking foe (e.g., Captain Froshus) gets it.

Oh yes, also I must wind up the automatic botty-booter you sent and bend over. Good idea, I think Yeller and Normus might come back for a demonstrayshun of that. Yeller likes trick machines, and Normus likes doing pain on people.

Yours ouchly,

Ivor Bootedbottom
(get it?)

Dear Mom and Dad,

Arrroooo! This morning, Yeller and Normus came out of their hidey-hole rushingly to watch the botty-booter go doof-doof. Yeller thinks it is quite good, a little like the chin-tickler he made out of a lectric fan 1 time. Only his machine was more har-hary than ouch-ouchy. Yeller wanted to take the botty-booter apart with his screwdriver, but Normus said it was rubbish and booted it back (jealous). Now it is up near Windy Ridge, I bet.

They both say Not Fair that they cannot Run Away to Sea with me to find the treasure. But I *think* they *know* deepdownly that they must stay here. Hope so, because who else will protect Smells xcept them when I go?

Guess what? Yeller had a big idea just now!
He said we must make Pirate Rules and do ship
training on Lake Lemming for the practiss of sea
habits. Arrroooo! All because he had read
LOADS about pirates. He did not say so before
because of being in a bad mood.

Yours studyingly,

Concrete Slab (for parking sheds on), Garden

Dear Mom and Dad,

I have made you a nice pic of us dressed up as
pirates on the small ship we just built. Our
ship is a bit cheap because of being made
out of an old shed and garden tools. But good
costumes, hmmm?

Dear Mom and Dad,

Today we did a launch of the good ship *Sheddy,* and off we went for a fine sail by Coot Island. It is up at the reedy end of Lake Lemming, in case you did not know.

It took *Sheddy* a long time because of going in circles, banging into things, etc. Shame about bears being heavy. Because if you are the steerybear, you have to sit by the rudder at the back end. Meaning, Normus tips up me and my crew in the air. So it's hard for him to sail straight (cannot see).

49

Also, he gets grumpy about us saying all the time, "Watch out, Normus. Go this way, no go that way." It says in Yeller's book what steerybears are s'posed to do if they want to do Going Around (e.g., turn around the other way).

Number 1 is point where you want to go and shout out, "Stand by to Go Around!" Number 2 is just before the sail comes flying over the other side, shout out "Lee Ho" (piratese meaning "Duck").

Our sail keeps being 2 quick. It comes over whizzingly and hits him. So Normus goes, "Hey! Stop that!" and hits it back. Now it is even more holey than from Smells shooting it. Boo, shame.

Sad to say, we did a big crash into Coot Island.

But 1 good thing, we did SST (Surprise, Speed, and Terror) after all, because then many coots hopped off flappingly doing loud cooty noises! Plus we did that without even trying. Good eh?

Arrrrooooo!

Yours hoyoyoly,

Little Wolf, P.C.

(Clue: not Police Constabull, not Personal Computer, not Piece of Cheese. Want to guess?)

Dear Mom and Dad,

More pirate practiss this morning, just after sunjumpup, but no luck capturing pirate victims. There are not many of them around Lake Lemming, only ducks, but they're 2 quick for us. Boo, shame. I love roast duck, kiss, kiss. Wunce, we were

creeping up on a pelican, saying (piratey voice), "Heave ho, matey. Hand over your beakful of fish, or we'll sink you. A-harrr!" But, not fair, he just gave me a sharp peck on the nose. And he swallowed Yeller's trick sword that he made.

We had a fine lunch. It says in Yeller's book about how pirates like eating crackers with weevils in them. We did not have many crackers, but not to worry. There are plenty of weevils tucked up in the cracks of the *Sheddy* (nice and juicy, yum, yum!). That got our strongness up for being Terrors. So up with our anchor and up with our sail, and off we went rockingly.

Quite soonly, we came to the north shore. Stubbs was at the front being the Lookout. He said, "ARK!" times 3, meaning "H*ark*, mateys! Otters l*ark*ing about off the st*ark*board bow!"

Yeller yelled, "AHOY YOU LUBBERS. LET US TRY YOUR MUDSLIDE A-HARRR, OR YOU SHARRL BE GETTIN A TASTE OF CHILLY STEEL!" But they just swam underwater and bot our ship's bittom (other way around, sorry).

Yours sunkly,

Little Glugglug

Dear Bubb add Dadd,

I hab got a small cold id
by doze, shame eh? It is all
those otters' fault for
making us get sunk. Normus likes going in the
water because of his hobby (trout tickling). But,
it makes me and Yeller go ~~hallerjick~~ ~~oo-ergic~~ all

funny. Still, we are not
giving up, so arrroooo!
times 3 for our braveness.
Plus arrrrooo to Stubbs
for cooking us some nice
warm micemince tarts 2 eat
(only he calls them t*ark*s).

Here is some more cheery news.
Normus found a punt in the cattails. Do
you know punts? They have a flat bottom,
and you push them by a pole (no sails), so
handier for pirately SST practiss
on ducks.

Only 1 prob. Smells has been down in the cellar. He found a short, fat, old musket of Uncle Bigbad's, a rusty old flintlock pistol, and gunpowder. He hates playing air guns now. He only wants to shoot blunderbusses.

We said he could tie the blunderbuss on the front of the punt (or is it frunt of the pont?) if he didn't do 2 many bangs.

More later.

Yours ah-choooly,

Diddle Boolf

P.S. Sorry about the sneezy bits (chewed micemince).

Under 4 Doovay Covers, My Bed, My Room

Dear Mom and Dad,

I am having to write this quietly (tickly throat plus ache in my head).

We did pirate practiss in the punt yesterday. It was bad because of Smells putting a whole cupful of gunpowder up his musket in 1 go. Not funny, because we were punting along, nice and creepingly, up to some tasty ducks riding on the water.

Normus did not sit on the back end this time. He had to lie down instead. Then he held up a mirror, so he could see the way to steer, and he did the rudder part with his back feet. Yeller and Stubbs had to skwash down on top of him, no wiggling. I did the poling job. Smells did being Gunner at the front.

I wanted to shout, "Heave 2, you ducks. Pirates here. Surrender 4 nice eggs, no fooling!" but my voice went wrong. It was so weaky with my cold, it would not come out of its hole. So quick as a chick, Smells did a command, saying, "Wings up, ducks. BANG!" Like that with his blunderbuss—only louder.

That bang made our punt rush back rocketly across the lake! Then bonk into a willow tree and splash into the wetness wunce morely.

Yours streamingly,

The Patient

P.S. Smells never misses.

P.P.S. Now I have a coff. Thanks, Smells, very much.

P.P.P.S. I am sending you a tape of my coff going kuh, kuh, kuh, kuh, in case you do not believe me.

Dear Mom and Dad,

Today me and Stubbs did *proper* Running
Away to Sea! Normus and Yeller
helped me pack my
knapsack with
snacks, etc. I am
~~in disgizz,~~
~~disgize~~ (still
cannot spell it)
wearing my
pretend pirate
costume:
eyepatch, peggy
leggy, etc. Also, Stubbs
has red and yellow
paint on (like a parrot). He can say "ARK!"
meaning Pieces of *Ark*. Get it? He is a good
parrot.

Smells is tucked up
sulkingly in his cot,
covered in spots. It might
be the chickypox from

eating 2 many chickies. Yeller and Normus say, yes, they will look after him. BUT (big but) I think they are grumpy underneath because of me not letting them come on our xciting search. They hate me again, I bet.

No more coff, no more reading, no more pirate practiss, just danger for me and Stubbs. Hope you are happy now. Also, this is my last letter probly. So a dew! (French)

Yours runawaytosealy,

Able Seawolf Little

Dear Parents of Little Wolf,

Bad **N**ews. I am not killed yet. (Wait, that is not the Bad News, sorry. I just put the Bad News part down 1st. It took me a long time doing the big B and the N, so I forgot my real news.) Do not fret and frown, the real Bad News is coming up next. Here it is for you. Ready, go.

Bad News (real). Smells has ~~dissobay~~ ~~disobb~~ not done what you said he must do. You know he went to bed with the chickypox? Well, that was not him. That was his teddy. Smells just tucked his teddy up in his cot and plopped red dots on him. He got the red dots with my best clicky pen that he knows he is not s'posed to touch, in case he might wear it out! I think he robbed that from me when he had that craze about being a burgle-arrr, remember?

That is how I found out
about him being a
stowaway in my
knapsack.
Something
kept going
clicky-click all
the time, in
between my peggy
leggy going kerlonk,
kerlonk down the
road. It was Smells!

Anyway, it is nice having my clicky pen back,
even if I do have to take Smells with me now to
seek Blackfur's treasure, etc. If I do not, you will
say moaningly that I am a slow, sluggy slowcoach
for not Running Away to Sea faster.

Yours zoomingly,

Little Russia (like rusher, get it?)

P.S. Stubbs says "ARk!" meaning he is
arkay.

Dear Mom and Dad,

Sorry about no letters for 3 days. We just kept
on rushingly, right through Hazardous Canyon
(2 much rushy water, brrr), then under
Funder Falls (wet paws all the time, plus soggy
peggy leggy, boo, shame). Next, we went across
the south part of the White Wildness. Wun time
we got snow white all over, but it was not funny.
Also we got sore bits from frostnip that the wind
did (by throwing sharp sleet at us crossing
the Razorback).

Then up jumped the sun when we got near
the coast. It was not turned up to its hottest,
but it made us a lot more cheery. We followed
the coast northly until we nearly got to the end
of Grimshire. Then we came to a cliffy
part on the south side of Noname Bay,
just by Wetness-on-Sea. Next, we had a
lie-down in the warm grass, hmmmm nice.

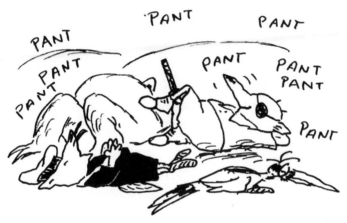

Then, after a lovely pant, plus watching some
ships going past on the sea, down we marched
watchingly into the little town, saying a
marching poem:

"Blackfur's treasure, we are after you.
Captain Froshus, watch out 2.
Grrr, grrr, grrr,
Plus, a loud Arrrrrooooo!"

Do you like our trick pic? It is not of fat ladies. It is really of me, Smells, and Stubbs.

Wetness is nice for wolves. Plus, Stubbs likes all the gulls going "EEEEK." He says they are *ark*ceptional. My peggy leggy got 2 hot, so off I popped it into my knapsack for now. My eyepatch is still on, just in case.

Smells likes the sea. It is all blue and wet—a little like Lake Lemming, only somebody put a load of salt in it. Spit, spit! The sand is nice 2. It is good for burying. Just our luck, because guess what Smells's new hobby is? Digging!

Yours uptomyneckly,

L.

P.S. No pirates around here.

Whizzland, Peppermint Rock Lane, Wetness-on-Sea

Dear Mom and Dad,

Stubbs and I wanted to get tracking today. Stubbs kept saying cawingly, "ARK!" times 4, meaning let us get b*ark* on the tr*ark* of the treasure of Bl*ark*fur and take it b*ark* to where it belongs. But Smells made us go to Whizzland, the amusement park. He went SCreamy SCream SCream until we spoiled him rotten.

We dug a hole under Whizzland's fence to get in. (We had no money.) Guess where we

came up? The Ghostie Train Tunnel. It was funny. We won the game because we were the

scariest. When we popped up, all the people went, "Help, mommy, ooo-er!" Then off they ran screamingly, har, har!

The roller coaster was funny 2—if
you love being sick like Smells does.
But my favorite was the Flea Circus.
It had flea ballet dancers with feathers
on, fleas pulling chariots,
fleas riding their bikes, etc.

I said to the circus man, "Do
you have Flea Wrestling?" He
said replyingly, "No." So
me and Smells went scratchy-
scratch in our fur, and I said,
"You have now!"
Out jumped a
small pack of our own
fleas. They ran into the ring
hoppingly to give those circus
fleas a good fight!

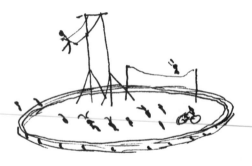

We thought that was the best part, but the man was cruel, saying, "Hey, buzz off you itchy wolves and take that scrawny parrot with you!"

Stubbs said, "ARK!" meaning do not be s*ark*y about parrots. That was a good insult for a short crow, yes? Then guess what? We won a goldfish. Yum, yum, tasty. It was on the Test Your Strongness with a Big Hammer game. We were a bit 2 weaky at 1st. We could not make the dinger go up and hit the bell. But then Stubbs sat on it. So the next time we hit with the hammer, Stubbs did just 1 small flippy-flap. Up he went and hit the bell with a loud donk!

DONK

But that winning-a-goldfish trick was not Y we got kicked out of Whizzland, oh no! It was because of Smells winning all the dollies at the shooting gallery. He hit bull's-eye, bull's-eye, bull's-eye. He never misses.

So now we are off to the harbor to look for Blackfur clues. No ~~sine sing~~ sign of unicorns in bays yet or of people having an itch. Maybe that song was a just a pretend 1? Remember?

> *Seek my treasure in the bay,*
> *Where the unicorn doth play!*

We are being very careful and hiding from anywun who looks like Captain Froshus and smells of pepper.

Yours dollieduply,

L. W.

Below Deck, The Saucy Sardine,
Somewhere on the Shivery Sea

Dear Mom and Dad,

You know we went down to the harbor? Well that is a fancy name for a place where they keep fishing boats on leashes. So I thought, hmmm, good place to go when Running Away to Sea. Also, to find out what tricks Captain Froshus has been up to, so we can think of a better way to SCARE him, if he finds the treasure before us.

Soon we saw a boat painted green (my favorite color). Plus, it had a nice name, **The Saucy Sardine.** Also, it had a big sign, saying:

So up the gangplank we went, saying, "Ahoy," etc., to the small, cheery man mending his fishing net. He said to us, "Ahoy there, mateys. What be you doing aboard *The Saucy Sardine*? I be the skipper, by the way."

So I said (sailory voice), "Good joke, matey, because where be your skipping rope?" But then he said, "Oh no, I be the *captain*." So *I* said, "Me and my pals here, we be looking for work."

The captain said, "That do make a nice change. Most deckhands are too scared to sign on for a voyage because of that Captain Froshus and his wicked crew."

I said, "We be not scared, matey, we be tuff. And, we be not deckhands, ah-harrr. But if you be looking for deck*paws,* then we have got strong wuns. Plus, my parrot pal here has got a strong deck*beak.* Also, I have got my own peggy leggy in this knapsack!"

So the captain said, "Well, nibble me ratlines— I like the cut of your jibs! I be Captain Bold, so welcome aboard. Now jump to it lively and stow your dunnage! We sail on the afternoon tide."

Yours crewly,

A. Fisher (get it?)

P.S. I found out "dunnage" is a sailor word for "stuff," good, eh?

Pointy End, The Saucy Sardine,
Not Far Away from Lurking
Rock Lighthouse, Shivery Sea

Dear Mom and Dad,

It is good being a deckpaw if you do not mind scrubbing decks or getting many a skwirt from Smells doing the hosing. Captain Bold is a good teacher. He likes having us around saying, "Eye-eye, Captain," then helping with stowing, steering, heave-hoes, up-she-rises, swabbing, etc.

Smells and I are good at cleaning out fish barrels. This is how we do it. Jump in a barrel, do a hedgehog curl-up, then a spinny-spin. We

are so quick, you would not bel*eeeeev*! Also, Stubbs is brilliant at mending nets with his clever beak. He keeps saying, "ARK! ARK!" meaning netw*ark*ing is *ark*cellent fun.

Catching sardines from boats is good. You catch them by a trick that is so *easy cheesy*! 1st you just throw a big net over the back on a long, strong string. Then all the fishes go, "Hmm, swimming in all this sea is 2 boring. Come on, let's have a challunj and try wiggling through those teeny-weeny holes. Oh no, help, my fins are stuck, boo, shame." So now double helpings of grub for us, Arrroooo!

You know that far part on the end of the sea where the sky comes down? That is called the horizon. It has a handsome sailing ship on it.

Yours spottingly,

Sharpeye

A Barrel, the Hold, The Saucy Sardine,
Somewhere on the Shivery Sea

Dear Mom and Dad,

Ooo-er, you know that handsome sailing ship?
Up it sailed swiftly, quiet as a cat. Captain Bold
said mutteringly, "What be that lubber's game? If
she don't watch it, she'll find herself all a-hoo
and tangled in our net! Quick boys, get out the
Signals Book and check them fancy flags she's
a-flying."

So quick as a chick, I checked, saying,
"Eye-eye, Skipper, that signal means
Have a Nice Day!"

"Arrr well, she be only one of
them thar pleasure schooners,"
said Captain Bold. "Yers,
I can see now. There be
crowds of jolly folk aboard
sucking caramel apples and
fizzypops and a wearing Kiss-
Me-Quick cowboy hats. Brace
yerselves, mates, while I ups the throttle
to Full Speed Ahead and steams out of her way."

Then off we went racingly with lines of white water coming out the back of us. But we could not leave that schooner behind, not even with our throttle at the top speed.

Captain Bold called out, "Has she come 'round far enough for you to make out her name yet, Mister Lookout?" So Stubbs said, "ARK!" times 3, meaning *Ark-ark* Captain, the name of that schooner is . . . **The Seafarkx!**

"Well, stap me in the scuppers and swab me sideways! Look-ee thar!" cried Captain Bold swearingly.

So we looked thar and oh no! Off came the seaside clothes and the Kiss-Me-Quick hats. Away went the caramel apples, down came the fancy flags, up went the covers, out came the cannons, and up went . . . the Snarl and Wishbones.

Ooo-er, pirates!!!

Yours hidinginabarrelly,

2 Deckpaws and 1 Deckbeak

Dear Mom and Dad,

Today was a busy 1. We did flying. Then we did more hiding. Then we did getting caught.

The flying part was in the barrel we were hiding in. The pirates thought our barrel must be just full of fishes like the others, so they picked us up with a winch (strong pickupper) and dropped us down their hold (ship's tummy). I said whisperingly to Smells and Stubbs, "No noise, in case they come searching, OK?"

I wanted us to wait until nighttime and then creep out in the deep dark. But all of a suddenly we heard taptap taptap. It was some pirates having a gloat over their new booties. 1 of them said (weaselly voice), "Yum, yum, Crusher, grilled sardines for supper tonight!"

Then the other 1 said wildboarly, **"We shall have a rare old party, Bluetooth. The cap'n says we can help him toast old Bold's toes after! Course, that's only for spite, seeing as he says he still knows nothing of Blackfur's treasure. Snort the man and snort again that we're no nearer finding it! But we shall toast Cap'n Bold's snorting toes just the same and then heave him over the side."**

Then they did a taptap on our lid, and Smells said, "Be quiet, Mister Tappyhead!" So the pirates said, "Hoy! Oo zed dat?" So Smells said, "Not me, it was the naughty fishes!" So cubbish.

They took off our lid and grabbed us harshly by our scruffs, saying, "Ah-harrr stowaways. Gotcha! Slam 'em in the snorting brig, etc."

Then we got locked up the pirate way (e.g., in irons).

Yours chaineduply,

Little

P.S. Never mind, they have not found Blackfur's treasure yet, have they?

Dear Mom and Dad,

Do you know brigs? You find them downstairs in pirate ships. They are nice and dark and smelly. They are a bit like dens (no portholes), only you put captured creatures in them. They have a strong iron door with nice big locks and bars. BUT (big but) they are a bit boring because you cannot get out of them.

You do not get fed tasty grub in the brig, only old bread and water,  yuck. Good thing there is many a lost rat down here. Lots of them do not know the Small Cave Trick. Along they come scuttlingly, saying (skweeky voice), "Hello, we are looking for the bilge, can you show us where it is?"

So we say, "Yes, go in this small cave, but be careful of all the stalagmites and tites. They are sharp." Then they pop in your mouth, so you can just go chomp. Hmmm, tasty.

SPLOOSH

Not much else happened today, only *an* then a *cheer* and a
BANG BANG BANG
I did not like those bangs. Loud noises by guns, etc., are the worst thing. So Stubbs said to me "ARK!" times 2, meaning do not fret and frown, that was only to cheer Captain Bold for getting ch*ark*ed over the side I *ark*spect.

Then Smells got a bit whiny. He likes being chained up, but he likes watching people getting splooshed better. So he went S C r e a m y S C r e a m S C r e a m, like always when he wants to be spoiled rotten. Then Crusher poked his snout through the bars. He is a tuff old boar, did I tell you that? He has a fat head, sharp tusks, and big shoulders like a moose. Also, he has SNORT tattooed on his forehead.

He thinks that makes him look 2 millium times fiercer, I bet. He said, **"Shut your snorting traps, you lubbers, or you'll end up swabbing out Davy Jones's locker!"** So rude.

I wonder who Davy Jones is. Also, I never knew lockers needed swabbing.

Yours interestedly,

Littly

Dear Mom and Dad,

Small Arrroooo! for being out of the brig but not 3 loud wuns, because I think Captain Froshus is going to make us dead.

After our bread-and-watery breakfast, Crusher opened up the iron door, saying, "Snort, look lively, you snorting captives. Smarten up. You are off to see the cap'n, snort." Then he threw a bucket of water over us, saying, "Bath time, 1st!" Sad to say, that cruel bucket of water made Stubbs's parrot paint come off. Plus, it washed off my eyepatch and made Smells's mustache crooked.

Then Bluetooth the Weasel made us do Stickup Paws with his pistols. So up onto the top deck we clanked drippingly (wet chains), then along came a bunch of pirates saying, "Har, har, you have had it now, etc."

But we did not go all wobbly and weakly, oh no! Up went my chin in the wolfly way and out went Smells's tongue going pppth, ppppth. Stubbs said, "ARK!" meaning I am not scared of Davy Jones, even if he has the d*ark*est l*ark*er ever. We went right up the back of the ship until we came to a fancy oak door. Crusher shouted, "Prisoners, halt!" going taptap with his ~~nkuckle~~ nuckle (cannot spell it) on the sign saying:

CAPTAIN'S CABIN

Crusher opened the door and pushed us all in. We could not see much in that cabin, only spoons and glasses flashing on the table and a tall shadowy brute behind it. He was standing in front of a wide window, wide as the ship, and the sunshine was bouncing off the waves blindingly.

Quick as a chick, I remembered Uncle Bigbad's Wolf Rule of Badness Number 3: *Fib your head off.* So I said (piratey voice), "At your service, C-Cap'n Froshus, a-harrr!"

Then I smelt a peppery smell. A soft voice said, "My boys, welcome aboard *The Seafox*, the quickest, slickest pirate ship afloat."

Then the voice said, "I am the notorious Captain Froshus. My mission is to be the All-time Terror of the Shivery Sea and to find the lost treasure of Blackfur the Backbiter. Something tells me that you know things about him that are unknown to me. Remember, I show no mercy to any who cross me or stand in my way. So, pay attention, my boys. Look deep, deep into my eyes. Can you really be of service to me, or are you just spies? Think carefully. The answer you give will determine whether you sail with me or swim with the sharks!"

Yours thisisitly,

Little Fibber

Cupboard (where they keep buckets, mops, etc.),
Up the Pointy End, The Seafox

Dear Mom and Dad,

Good thing his eyes were in the deep shadow.
It was so hard not to give in to Froshus. But I
tried my hardest, saying, "Good joke about spies,
Cap'n! Me and my brother plus my parrot here,
we be not spies, a-harrr. We be all harsh young
sailors wanted by the Coast Guard, grrr. We
stowed away on *The Saucy Sardine* just so you
might capture us and let us be in your crew
while treasure seeking, etc.!"

Bluetooth said whiningly, "A
bit small for outlaws, ain't you,
matey? And how come your
parrot looks more like a
scrawny little crow after his
bath!"

Stubbs said a brave "ARK!
ARK!" meaning Pieces of
Ark! Pieces of *Ark*! But
Bluetooth's big friend,
Crusher, said, "Snort!

What shall we do with them, skipper—heave 'em over the side and use 'em for target practice like we dun with Captain Bold?" Ooo-er.

But Captain Froshus spoke softly, saying, "My boys, you look a little pale. Not surprising after your ordeal in the brig. Please accept my apologies. I am surrounded by ruffians with appalling manners. Allow me to offer you a nourishing snack. I trust, being desperate young brutes and wanted sea outlaws, that you can be persuaded to accept treats from a stranger? Would anyone like to tell me all their secret information about Blackfur's treasure and help themselves to a bull's-eye . . . ?"

Bull's-eyes are Smells's favorite treat, so he said, "Me Me Me!" Then Captain Froshus said replyingly, "What an eager young chap you are in your handsome sailor suit. And what an impressive mustache, if a little lopsided. Young sir, in return for a pawful of bull's-eyes and the promise of a job as my personal cabin cub, what are you prepared to tell me?"

Answer, "Everything."

So now Smells is cabin cub and cook's helper, all because of getting bribed! Stubbs must leave my shoulder and be the lookout in the Crow's Nest. It is right at the top of the tallest mast, miles 2 high up for him, I bet. And guess what job I have got? Captain Froshus said I could be the head cleaner. Good, I like bossing people around.

Still, it will not be long before Smells blabs all of our secret clues about Blackfur and about how he is our great ancestor. Plus, all about our portrait of him with his chest and his twisty stick and about that old Blackfur song you sent. Smells kept playing it on his Walkwolf, so I bet he hasn't forgotten it.

Seek my treasure in the bay,
Where the unicorn doth play!
Those who seek without a map,
Mind the teeth that snarl and snap!
Lucky those who most do itch,
Scratch and lo, ye shall be rich!

So adieu wunce morely. Soon it will be cheer,

sploosh, bang, bang, bang, over the side for us, I bet. Then Captain Froshus will get so rich, all the people will say, "Captain Froshus is the Best Terror of All Time. He makes great wolves like Blackfur Wolf and Bigbad Wolf seem like tame weakies!"

Yours shamedly,

Little Wolf (not great, sniff)

P.S. They were not even real bull's-eyes. They were just a trick, e.g., mint candies with stripes, yuck.

P.P.S. I have just found out another trick. I am the cleaner of the head, not the head cleaner. Sad to say, the head is the sailor word for the bathroom, so that is me pinned up.

Dear Mom and Dad,

I am sooooo tired, phew. It has been scrub,
scrub, scrub in the Head and pirates calling me
names all the time. Also, the wind got up early (it
was sleeping behind Vile Isle). Then it found some
rain to throw while giving the sea a shake, so all
the pirates keep shouting out chantingly,

*Lubber,
the Scrubber,
we have been sick!
Fetch
your bucket
and mop here quick!*

Big fuss today because of Stubbs not wanting to stay in the Crow's Nest (2 giddy). He keeps hopping down the rigging to the crosstrees (sticks holding out the sails), saying, "ARK!" meaning he wants to be the larkout from lower down. Now the boatswain is after him to give him a sting with a short rope.

Captain Froshus has been trying and trying to get treasure clues from Smells by spoiling him rotten. I can see the steering wheel now, and guess who is getting to try steering? Smells!

Also, not fair, he has got on a big waterproof hat and cloak, so he can copy Captain Froshus and the mate by looking cool and mysterious.

Now the captain and the mate are having a huddly look at the sea map, with hats pulled down darkly. The captain is saying to Smells, "Sing us your funny song, my boy! Then the nice mate and I can look on the chart and see if there are any places that match the words. If you are a helpful young chap, you shall get a share of the treasure and be rich. Then you can buy a splendid little pirate ship of your own."

Smells says replyingly, "ᗷ ᴑ ᴑ ᴍ ᖯ ᴑ ᴑ ᴍ ᖯ ᴑ ᴑ ᴍ !" So Captain Froshus says, "Absolutely, my boy. You shall also have as many cannons as you wish. Now sing!"

I will just pop this letter in a bottle for you (2 wet) and start up another 1 quick.

Yrs hastingly,

L.

92

Dear Mom and Dad,

Good thing Smells is terrible at singing. Because, when he sings the Blackfur song, it comes out like this:

Unicorns got the treasure,
Don't wanna play.
Snap snarl bay,
Sickee, sickee, sickee,
Itchy, Itchy Richy.

Now Captain Froshus is saying whisperingly to the mate, "Mostly cubbish nonsense, of course, but can you see a Snarl Bay on the chart? Or what about Itchy Point? Or Unicorn Something?"

Smells is not paying attention because he's having a nice time singing. Plus, steering the ship, going b rrr m b rrr m.

Aha! Now the mate has seen something on the chart. He said, "There be a group of rocky islands here, Cap'n, a day or two's sailing to the east of Vile Isle. There be Parrot Island, Piggy Island, and Narwhal Island. And here be a Narwhal Bay, look. No sign of Unicorn Island, though, Cap'n."

Now Captain Froshus is acting all fed up and snappish. Oh no! Here comes the boatswain, with Stubbs under 1 arm, saying, "Mutiny! This young crow be too scared to stay up in the Crow's Nest as ordered, Cap'n!"

Guess what the captain just said snarlingly? He said, "All paws and hoofs on deck to witness punishment! We shall have to teach this young coward a lesson. Fifty lashes should do the trick! Fetch the cat-o'-nine-tails!"

Yours mustdosomethingly,

Little

Dear Mom and Dad,

Sorry if this paper is even ~~smujjier~~ ~~rinklier~~
~~wetter than before~~. I have just found out what
"welking the plonk" is, Dad. And all because I
did not want Stubbs getting lashes from a cat
with nine tails.

All the pirates came up on deck, saying, "Oh
good, it has almost stopped raining. We have not
seen a nice flogging all week." Then along came
the boatswain. He tied Stubbs to the ship's
rail harshly, saying, "I be
going to give you a taste of
the cat-o'-nine-tails, my
bird!" What a whopping
big fibber about
cats! He did
not have a
cat, just a
whip
with nine
strings and
~~nkots~~ ~~nots~~
knots on it.

Then the sun bit a hole in the clouds, the drums went brrrr, and up went the boatswain's strong right hand with the whip ready. So I jumped springingly onto the quarterdeck. I got out my Cub Scout knife and cut Stubbs's ropes, saying, "Fly for it, Stubby! You can do it!" Down came the whip crackingly, but not quick enuff for a quick crowchick! Up went Stubbs flappingly. Bang, bang, bang, bang went the anti-air crow guns, but Stubbs zigged off zaggingly, saying, "ARK!" times 3, meaning bad l*ark*. I have *ark*scaped. You missed the m*ark*!

Sad to say, I did not *ark*scape. All the pirates grabbed ahold of me, saying, "Let us feed this 1 to the sharks, Cap'n. Please or we shall not be having no cruel fun at all today."

So the captain said softly, "Very well, you shall have your wicked way. Little Wolf—for I know it is he—is of no further use to me, and his baby brother is now entirely in my power. It is only a matter of time before Blackfur's treasure is mine! Over the side with the little brute and good riddance." Then he took off his yellow waterproof hat all of a suddenly and let me see his pointy face. Oh no, he was not Captain Froshus—he was Mister Twister the Fox!

Then the pirates made me stand on a short floorboard sticking over the side. I looked down, saying, "Hey, not fair! That is a long drop, and look at all those sharks down there!" But they did not pay any attention. They made me do a long walk, hurryingly, by pricking my bottom with sharp points. Ooooch, ouch, splooosh!

Yours nomorely,

Mister Ghostiecub

Smells did th

Dear Mom and Dad,

Good thing Smells got all jealous about me
going sploosh. He wanted to have a sploosh 2.
In he came splooshing on top of me in the salty
water, holding the little wooden spoon that he
got for being cook's helper.

← Smells did th

← Smells did th

Around and around us circled a pack of
hungry sharks. They showed us their big teeth
just to make us go all froze and stiff, I bet. But I
said, "Back to back, Smells. We will show these
sea wolves how land wolves can fight!" Then
Smells and I made a whopping splash, saying
sternly, "Shove off you big bullies, or you will
all get a harsh thwack on the nose. No kidding.
Grrr!"

Smells did

Getting thwacked on the nose is a shark's worst nightmare. Did you know that? So, well done for tricky braveness! Then we saw the pirates leaning over the side shouting, "Snort and blust it! The blinking blunkers be still alive. Get the muskets! Run out the bow chaser! Target practiss!" Then it was BANG BANG BANG BANG bOOM for a bit. But they could not hit a flea, lucky for us. Plus, all of a soonly, the wind blew the other way and made them sail away from us. Arrroooo!

Away and away blew *The Seafox*. Then guess what? It fell off the edge of the sea. Arrroooo! Serves them right. So then there was just me and Smells left floating on top of the wide part of the sea. I said, "Smells, let's do a fast eastly swim. If we do not get eaten or drowned, maybe we will come to an island, yes?"

Smells did this.

Smells got all whiny, saying, "I hate sea. I only like pirate ships." So I said, "Never mind, Smells, and keep cubbypaddling until we come to some nice brown land. Then we can dig a small den to rest in. Plus, you can write on my letter if you like. I am sending this to Mom and Dad in my very last bottle, OK?"

Smells did th

So the nice writing is mine, and Smells did the cubbish skribbully bits.

Yours floatingly,

Little and Smells

P.S. We had to take the letter out of the bottle again to do a short P.S. P.P.S. The P.S. is that Stubbs has come back, Arrroooo! He went to look for land. He found some (not 2 far. as the crow flaps), but he is feeling arksauceted. So now he is sitting on my head guidingly.

Dear Mom and Dad,

Ooo-er! We keep getting almost killed, but not by sharks. By other sharp teeth!

Cubbypaddling is hard if you are only a small weaky like Smells. Also, even if you have tuff mussuls like me, hem, hem. Good thing I had Stubbs on my head, because every time my eyelids went click, he went "ARK!" meaning keep aw*ark*! Keep t*ark*ing.

But then we did not have the strongness in our legs for more kicking. I felt very down and dumply. But Stubbs flapped his wings, saying "ARK!" meaning h*ark*, pay *ark*tention. So we h*ark*ed. 1ˢᵗ we heard a RAAHH, like that, only soon it got more like a RAAAH.

You think it was lions or tigers, I bet? But no, it was big waves hurting themselves on sharp, black rocks. I said, "Wake up, Smells. Rocks! And there is an island on the other side of them. Arrroooo!"

Smells did not open his eyes. I said, "Do your cubbypaddle, Smells, else you might go under or get hurt on the rocks!" Just then I saw 2 big shadows coming up from deep down in the water. I thought, oh no, those sharks are crafty. They are waiting until we fall asleep. Then they will munch us up!

Stubbs said, "ARK!" meaning lookout, sharks! But then came a whistly voice, saying, "Hello, you furry boys. Hop onto our backs if you want a lift."

Yours holdingtightly,

Little Cowboy

Warm Sandy Beach (somewhere dry)

Dear Mom and Dad,

It was porpoises that picked us up on their backs, not sharks. They are such good swimmers, faster than ships, I bet. They are like sea Cub Scouts. They like doing a good deed every day (e.g., opposite of Uncle Bigbad's Rule of Badness Number 6, *Do your dirtiest every day*). Handy, huh?

The porpoises carried us straight for the rocks, doing their whistling. We thought, oh no, soon we will be like cubby kabobs on those sharp points! But no, those porpoises can dodge and jump about 1 millium miles high! Over some rocks we went flyingly. Also, we went through some gaps skweezingly—until we came into a bay. The nice porpoises set us down on the warm sand. We whistled bye-bye and, *zzz z z z z,* were fast asleep.

Morning time now. We are alive still— but macarooned!

Yours wide-eyedly,

The Wolf Bros
(plus Stubbs)

Dear Mom and Dad,

Here is my riddle for today (instead of boring news). What goes:

"*wsHHHHH wsHHHHH plop plop pinck pinck skwaark!?*"

Answer: an island.

Did you get it? The first part is waves. No, the next part is not rude. It is big hollow nuts going plop on your head if you sit under their trees for a cool-off. Next is crabs (tasty), and the last part is parrots, etc.

I am sitting on the sand having a hard think about what islands Captain Froshus's mate said he found on his chart.

Wun was Parrot Island. Then he said Piggy Island. Then there was a funny name but, sad to say, I cannot remember it.

So maybe this 1 we are on is Parrot Island. Or is it Piggy Island? We have not smelt any piggies yet, boo, shame. Maybe they live up the hill in the jungly part. Tomorrow I am going for a long *ark*splore with Stubbs.

Smells says he wants to stay on the beach and dig (his favorite thing, remember?). He is xcited because he found lots of old brown bottles in the sand saying RUM in old writing. They smell funny, a little like Uncle Bigbad's whisky bottle when he was a ghostie spirit.

But it is very good because bottles are handy for sending letters. Plus for bonking snacks on the head, e.g., crabs, limpets, winkles, nuts, etc.

Yours desertislandly,

The Castaway

Dear Mom and Dad,

Stubbs and I had a good old *ark*splore today.
Right up the top of the hill, I went in-and-out-
of-the-palm-treesly. Stubbs was teaching all the
parrots to say, "ARK!" It is easy cheesy for them
because they are quick copiers. If you say to
them, "Hello flashywings, say
inkywinkypinkybeak," they say it back.

When we got up to the top we could see all
around. So there you are, this is deffnly an island.
It is all green (my favorite color), with yellow
and black around the edges.

We spied another bay next
to ours. It looked like a small bite
out of the island. There
were many black rocks guarding
it, more than in our bay even.

We could just see a big something swimming in the water on the other side of those rocks. We thought, hmmm, a big fish, miles bigger than porpoises even. He was sliding along like a shadow, then diving down, then coming up for a gasp. So we thought, aha, a whale. But guess what? He had a huge, long, spiky spike sticking out of his face! I said, "Ooo-er, it's a seamonster!"

We called out to Smells to run around the edge of the island and look. He likes monsters. But he was 2 busy digging or 2 far away to hear.

There is not 1 smell of a piggy but plenty of wiggly snacks, kwite tasty. So I do not think this can be Piggy Island. Must be Parrot Island. Or that other island I have forgotten the name of.

Yours sherlockly,

The Figureitouter

Dear Mom and Dad,

I am writing this by misty moonlight—deep breath, steady, steady.

You will not beLEEEEV what Smells has dug up now! Lots of cannons, plus pistols, muskets, flints, tinderboxes with matches, gunpowder, cannonballs, small bullets, swords, etc. PLUS (big plus) lots of pirate costumes and blankets in a trunk! Arrroooo! Are these from our ancestor Blackfur the Backbiter? Maybe his treasure is somewhere on this island 2! Maybe this *is* the island with the funny name that we can't remember?

Smells went crazy digging in the sand all day, so holes *everywhere* around here. But still not 1 bit of gold or jewels yet. Boo, shame. Tomorrow we will go and dig next door in Monster Bay. (I made that name up, do you like it?) BUT (big but), even if we find the treasure, how can we get it home?

Yours still macaroonedly,

Littly

P.S. Good thing the gunpowder is damp. Smells has found out how to get sparks from a tinderbox. He wants to be Mister Clicky and blow it up all at wunce.

Monster Bay, Just Around the Corner from Our Bay,
Somewhere Island, Notsurewhat Sea

Dear Mom and Dad,

We woke up today—
still all misty. We had a
snack of sea urchins.
They're a bit like
hedgehogs only pricklier.
So it was bonk with a rum

bottle, then watch your paws and nose. Then off
we went paddlingly around the corner to the
next bay.

Smells came 2. He was
hoping we might see the
seamonster wunce
morely. We took pistols
tucked up our shorts.
But the gunpowder was
still damp so we had to
pretend to shoot, saying,
"Pchhh, pchhhh, got you.
Roll over, you are dead."

It was kwite hard seeing (mist). So when we got to that next bay, we could not see the rocks. Stubbs said, "ARK!" meaning let us try an *ark*speriment of doing a whistle in the water through a hollow bamboo. Then maybe those kind porpoises would come and help. For instance, we could ask, "Has the seamonster got any bad hobbies?" Answer, "Yes, he likes eating macarooners, etc."

Just then the mist started melting. Smells pointed out to the sea, saying, "Look, pirates coming. Ppchhh, pchhh, you are dead!" We had a long look, and yes, there was a sailing boat coming. It was only a small sailing 1. You will think, "Good, it was not *The Seafox* then." Ah, but it *was* flying the Snarl and Wishbones!

I said, "Down flat, everybody, and no going pchhhh, Smells! We must hide out of the way, in case of cannonballs!"

The boat pointed itself at the rocks, trying to find a way through them. Down came the sail and then—

"ARK!" said Stubbs, meaning seamonster Att*ark*!

All of a zoomingly, the seamonster came up out of the water like a big rock come to life! He went crashingly over the waves, pointing his sharp spike at the side of the boat! We shouted out "Arrroooo!!" and "ARK!" and danced because of being saved from the pirates. Then **BASH!**, the seamonster went flying out of the water!

Around he went spinningly, with half of his spike knocked off. Then down he dived, all shamed.

That was when the boat went **CRUNCH** onto the rocks.

Yours shockedly,

Littly

Dear Mom and Dad,

It's boring today. Not really, only joking! there weren't pirates in that boat. It was Normus Bear and Yeller coming to help us!!

Normus was the 1 who grabbed hold of the seamonster's spike when it was about to sink the boat. Also, when he gave the seamonster a hard hit, half the spike broke off in  his paw. So the seamonster went back down to the deep going, "Boohoo, blub, blom, I want my mom." Normus gave the spike to Yeller for a present. Sad to say, then the boat got stuck on the rocks. Into the seawater jumped Normus with Yeller on his back. Strong as King Kong, he came swimmingly to the shore, right up to us!

Out of the water they rushed with a shake and a splash. We were all so happy we had a fun wrestle, even Stubbs. I said, "Arrroooo! I thought you 2 were angry with me 4 leaving you behind."

But Yeller yelled, replyingly, "DO NOT BE SILLY, LICKLE! WE ARE YOUR PALS. WE WOULD NEVER LET YOU DOWN."

Then we played chase and rolled in the sand until our panting got so fast we could not speak. But then Stubbs said, "ARK!" meaning that the seamonster's spike was *ark*zactly like Blackfur the Backbiter's walking stick.

Yeller said, shouting, "YES, THAT WAS A CLUE IN BLACKFUR'S PORTRAIT." He also said that when he found out where that twisty stick came from, he found out what the 1st clue in the Blackfur song meant!

I will xplain that clue to you soonly by rum bottle. Also, I will say how he figured out what the Blackfur song means. But no more writing today, I just want to have FUN!

Your cheery boy,

Littly

Dear Mom and Dad,

Arrroooo! We are hot on the trail of Blackfur the Backbiter's treasure. Now I will say how.

You know when Stubbs and I had to Run Away to Sea swiftly, and Yeller and Normus were s'posed to stay and look after Smells? Well, as soon as they found out Smells was not in bed with the chickypox, Yeller had a good think. He thought, "HMMMM, WE MUST FIND SMELLS AND HELP LICKLE. WHICH WAY DID THEY GO?" Then he thought, "I KNOW! LICKLE HAS GOT A SHARP DETECTY BRANE, SO SOON HE WILL BE ON THE TRAIL OF BLACKFUR THE BACKBITER'S TREASURE. I BETTER THINK UP A GOOD IDEA OF FINDIN A SHORTCUT, IN CASE LICKLE, SMELLS, AND STUBBS GET IN TROUBLE WITH CAPTAIN FROSHUS."

Then he had a long look at Blackfur's portrait. All of a suddenly, "DING! I KNOW WHERE I HAVE SEEN A TWISTY STICK LIKE BLACKFUR IS HOLDIN. IT WAS IN MY BOOK I WAS READIN CALLED *Shocking Brute Beasts of the Deep and Dark*. SO I WILL FLIP THROUGH THE PAGES. YES, THERE ARE FINE PICS OF WHALES. THERE ARE SPERM WUNS, KILLER WUNS, BLUE WUNS, etc. BUT (BIG BUT) THERE WAS A FUNNY WUN WITH A BIG, LONG SPIKE STUCK ON HIS FACE. THE WRITIN SAID UNDERNEATH:

THE NARWHAL OR SEA UNICORN

DING! IT SAYS ABOUT UNICORNS AND TREASURE IN BLACKFUR'S SONG!"

I said, "Aha, Yeller, I know the part you mean:

Seek my treasure in the bay,
Where the unicorn doth play!"

Then we had to let
Smells sing that song
in his funny way
about 1 millium
times—until he got
a coff.

Coff

Yours backinaminly,

I. M. Bustin (get it?)

Dear M and D,

Phew, phew, that's better. Sorry.

When it was all quiet, e.g., when Smells had stopped coffing, Normus said, "Yes, Yeller remembered the words in that part of the song too. So we got out a big map of Beastshire, Grimshire, and all the seas to look for narwhals or unicorns. And faraway to the east in the Sea of Sultriness, we found Narwhal Island and Narwhal Bay."

Yeller said, "YEAH. SO THEN WE WENT OFF QUICK AS A CHICK TO THE SHIVERY SEA, BORROWED A BOAT, AND SAILED HERE AS FAST AS WE COULD."

"It was my idea to fly the Snarl and Wishbones," said Normus proudly. "I know we are not pirates really, but I wanted the flag to say, *We only look small, but watch it, we are brute beasts!*"

"BIG SHAME, WE DID NOT HAVE A
REAL CHART OF NARWHAL ISLAND TO
SHOW US A WAY THROUGH THE ROCKS,
THOUGH!" Yeller yelled sadly.

"Aha! Those *rocks* are the teeth that snarl and
snap, I bet!" I said. Then I sang the clue from
Blackfur's song:

Those who seek without a map,
Mind the teeth that snarl and snap!

So, Mom and Dad, that means the *last* part of
the song has also got an important clue in it. But
now we are all having a nice lie-down on the
beach under the stars. Maybe after a good rest,
we will all wake up more clever.

Yours curledupcontently,

L. Wolf and Co. Ltd.

Narwhal Bay, Narwhal Island, the Sea of Sultriness

Dear Mom and Dad,

What a scratchy night we had. It was sand fleas. They made us go itch, itch all the time, boo, shame.

Those sand fleas got Normus's temper up. That is Y he got up very early and started pounding the sand, saying, "I hate Narwhal Bay! It is itchier than an itchy ants' nest!" That made Smells start copying him, by throwing sand all over.

Then all of a suddenly, Yeller and I went DING! together. Plus we started singing the last part of the song together.

Lucky those who most do itch,
Scratch and lo, ye shall be rich!

"I GET IT, LICKLE!" yelled Yeller. "THE CLUE MEANS YE MUST SCRATCH YE *SAND*, NOT SCRATCH YE *FUR*, IF YE WANT TO GET RICH!"

So we all went dig, dig in the sand of Narwhal Bay. It was hot work with the sun on our heads, but we did not stop. Then I felt a hard thing under my claws. I thought, "This is a big rock." But it was not a rock, it was a big chest.

Arrroooo! I howled to the others, and they all came and helped. We scratched and scratched in the sand until we could pull out that big chest! Normus gave the lock a hard bash. Up went the lid.

And look, I have made you a nice pic of us having a pretend bath with all the gold and jewels!

Yours gloatingly,

Little and
Chums

P.S. Only prob
is, how do we
get it back to
the den 4 you?
(No boat.)

Narwhal Bay, Narwhal Island, the Sea of Sultriness

Dear Mom and Dad,

It is nice being rich, but not if you are macarooned forever and ever. It is no fun having lots of jewels, etc., if you cannot ever go home and get your own bedroom wallpaper and have tons of scary fun in a real deep, dark forest.

So this is our plan. We are going to send a message to *The Seafox* saying:

Help Seafox, we ~~sfender, sufenda,~~ give up. We have found the treasure, and you can have it. BUT (big but) only if you take us back home to the far shore of Beastshire. P.S. Be nice, we are not many.

Good 1, yes?

Yours giveuply,

L., etc.

Dear Mom and Dad,

1 big prob about giving up. How do we get the message to Captain Froshus? (Mister Twister really.)

Answer: Stubbs!

His tail feathers that Smells plucked off him have grown back (mostly). So we said how about him flying to *The Seafox*, holding our message in his beak? That made him go all trembly. He said, "ARK?" meaning what about hurr*ark*anes and sh*ark*s, etc.?

I said, "Stubbs, you have been a fine fake parrot. Plus, you *ark*scaped from the pirates' anti-air crow fire. Plus, you guided me and Smells to Narwhal Island. I am your pirate chief saying, *Stubby Crow, you are a hero already. Plus, you are only small. So only go if you want to, OK?*"

Out went Stubbs's small chest. He said a soft
"ARK!" meaning *arkay* Chief, and do not be
~~wurrid,~~ worried, I will be b*ark*! And off he flapped
nobly over the rocks, until he was just like a small
period, e.g.

It is a bit windy, so paws crossed that he does
not crash into the Sea of Sultriness (sharks).

Yours hopingforthebestly,

Dear Mom and Dad,

Stubbs has been gone 4 many a bright moon. Maybe he is a bit 2 weaky to reach *The Seafox*. BUT (big but) me and my small pirate crew must get ready. I have made you a list of stuff we must do, just in the small case of Stubbs's wings having the strongness to flap him all the way to that ship with our message.

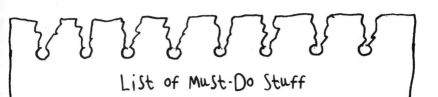

List of Must-Do Stuff

 Cannons. Drag (well, Normus mostly) the cannons, etc., around to Narwhal Bay.

Hide them under some old blankets (sand color).

Take tinderbox away from Smells for a short time, then finish drying the gunpowder.

Dress up in the old pirate clothes we found. Put on lots of swords, daggers, cutlasses (not cute lasses, Dad), pistols in belts made spesh to hold them. I get to wear the pirate cheef's (e.g., Blackfur's) costume: a hat with a bones badge made out of all sparkly jewels, earring, etc.

 Tuck fuses under my pirate hat for a big shock later.

 Me and Yeller and Normus put on boots with xtra thick soles.

 Jump skweezingly into our 3 biggest cannons for practiss.

ho ho Sing Ho yoyo, etc., a lot in loud whisper for practiss and crew spirit.

Arrroooo! Did you think, "Oh no, the shame. Our boy is going to surrender to Mister Twister?" I bet you did. But NO! That was a **Trick Message** we sent to trick him. But shhhh, so he doesn't find out.

Yours waitandseely,

Blackfur the Backbiter the 2nd, Pirate Chief

Dear Mom and Dad,

I am not saying "Har, Har," in case you might nip me sharply. But today we are glad I did not listen to you saying, "Grrrr, forget about reading and pirate practiss!" Because they helped a *lot*!

At sunjumpup we saw *The Seafox* sailing sneakingly up to the rocks—but not crashing. Boo, shame (big anchor). All the pirates were on deck looking for us. They could see the treasure chest on the beach, but not us hiding craftily under Blackfur's blankets.

Mister Twister spoke to us through his loudshouter, saying (soapy voice), "Ahoy there, my boys. Captain Froshus speaking. Where are you? Do not fret and fear. Come out and show yourselves! I have received and understood your message. Well done. How wise to surrender to me. I am, after all, the biggest Terror of All Time! Your messenger, the crow, is exhausted but safe. I have him tied to a hammock in my sick bay. He shall come to no harm. *Of course,* we shall be nice to *you,* provided there are no tricks. Wait where you are, while we lower a boat. We shall collect the treasure and then come back and collect you."

I whispered, "You will not trick us with your foxy ways, Mister Twister! Ready, Yeller? Ready, Normus? It is time to give him some SST! Stand by to remove blankets. Smells . . . GO!"

Off came the blankets and into the cannons we popped.

We could hear the pirates give a big loud laugh, thinking we were trying to hide like rabbits. They did not know about Surprise, Speed, and Terror waiting 4 them!

Yours whizzingly,

The Faymuss Furry Cannonballs

Dear Mom and Dad,

Good firing, Smells! He never misses!

Into the rigging flew us
furry cannonballs. All the
fuses under my hat were
smoking. Down I came
like a big scary cloud full
of thunder, shooting pistols
going "Graaaah!"

Out came my trusty Cub Scout penknife. Out
came Yeller's cutlass, and out came Normus's 2-
pawed sword. Down the ratlines we went,
swingingly with a slosh and a slash.
Snip went the ropes holding up
the sails. Normus was on the
deck swiftly, so he did
Swashing, Buckling, and
Bashing all around. BANG went
Bluetooth. BIFF went the
boatswain. CRASH went
Crusher. Then Sploosh, Sploosh,
Splooosh! All of them went over the side!

The rest of the pirates went "HELP, WHAT BE HAPPENING?" Because down came the sails on top of them. So:

1. They could not see proply.
2. They got tangled like sardines in a net.
3. When the cannons went off bang, they got a coff from the smoke.
4. They got a hard thwack by Normus, if they did not surrender quick!

Across the deck I came swingingly on a rope, saying (gruff voice), "Where be Captain Froshus or, should I say, Mister Twister the Fox? A-harrr! You have upset the wolfly spirit of the Greatest Terror of the Sea Ever. So here I be, the shocking spirit of Blackfur the Backbiter come to haunt you and your crew of cowardly custards!"

Your victorious pirate chief,

Little Seawolf

Dear Mom and Dad,

Do you know paw-to-paw combat? I have just had some with Mister Twister.

Normus and Yeller put all the pirate prisoners in lifeboats. Yeller shouted a good joke at them, "ROW AWAY AND DO NOT COME BACK!" Just then our gunner (Smells) started firing cannonballs that made whopping big splooshes near them in the water, so away they went swiftly like daddylonglegs.

Then up from the sick bay jumped Mister Twister, covered in armor. He had on a big iron helmet and an iron jacket plus iron pants to keep him safe.

He had a pistol in 1 paw, and Stubbs in the other, saying, "You may have fooled those miserable weasels and wild boars with your pistols and fizzing fuses, but you cannot fool a fox. I know you are *not* Blackfur the Backbiter, former Terror of the Shivery Sea. You are just that scrawny Little Wolf. Now hand over the treasure or say farewell to your crow friend."

I said gulpingly, "How about we fight paw-to-paw for Stubbs and the treasure instead?"

Mister Twister put Stubbs down, saying, "Certainly, my boy." Only he did not say that he would have a sword. And me, with only my Cub Scout penknife.

I said, "Be careful, my penknife has got a spiky thing for digging. Wait, it is a bit stiff."

But he would not wait fairly. He came rushing at me cheatingly with a swoosh, saying, "Take that, Master Backbiter!"

Just then Smells went **BANG** with his
blunderbuss from the beach. It was a long way
away. The musket ball went snip
through Mister Twister's suspenders.
Down went his iron pants, DONK!
I went rushingly up behind him
and gave him a sharp nip on the
you-know-what. Har, har!

Mister Twister went "EEEEEK!"
like a big baby mousy. Then he
went over the side. Splooosh!

Normus said, "Catch this life belt, Mister
Twister. Keep splashing, because look, a big shark
is after you!"

Yeller said, "GOOD WORK, LICKLE, OR
SHOULD I CALL YOU LICKLE BLACKFUR?"

Yours winningly,

LB the BB

*Fancy Table, Captain's Cabin, The Seawolf (hem hem),
the Shivery Sea, Near the Coast of Beastshire*

Dear Mom and Dad,

This is the last letter I am sending by bottle. My next 1 will be by envelope. Arrroooo!

Sad to say, you are not rich yet. No treasure 4 you. Y? Answer, here is a clue:

Guess who that small sailor is, cuddling the treasure chest? He is saying, "Hello all my darling gold and jewels, you are mine. Kiss, kiss." We had to let him be the owner, because he kept letting off all the cannons so our ears went ding. And you always say, "Give in to him. It is the only way." So we did.

Never mind. I 'spect you are happy about me getting back the proud name of Wolf by capturing a ship from a crafty fox, yes?

Here's a pic of us having a fine life on the ocean wave, on the good ship *The Seawolf* (our special new name, hem, hem). That is me being the captain. Normus is the 1 doing the fishing. Yeller is the 1 shouting, "I CAN SEE A MONSTER IN THIS TELESCOPE." (It is Stubbs looking at him down the other end really!)

Maybe Smells will bring his riches with him to the den if you let him come back and be your cabin cub. Only joking, not really. He wants to stay with me and Yeller and Normus and Stubbs *for ages*. Not just because he knows we are the best crew ever. It is because SST is Smells's favorite thing now. Plus he knows our Big Plan. I will say it to you in the next letter, if you like.

Yours temptingly,

Captain L. Wolf,
Terror of the Shivery Sea

Dear Mom and Dad,

Here is that something you are dying to know about, I bet.

The **Big** Plan

When me, Normus, Yeller, Stubbs, and Smells get to land, we are going to make a huge cart and put *The Seawolf* on it. Then we are going to push it all the way back to Frettnin Forest and launch it on Lake Lemming! Then we will call the big old house, that used to belong to Uncle Bigbad, Adventure Academy again. We will put up this sign saying:

Calling all slow weakies,
Come and learn SST (Surprise, Speed, and Terror)
from me and my faymuss pirate crew!
Have a free sail in the good ship SEAWOLF
that we captured from Captain Froshus
(Mister Twister).
Bags of Bangs, Clanks, Tricks, and Fun.
Signed, Little Blackfur

Arrroooo! for the pirate crew!

Shock on the Shivery Sea: Wolves Are Top Terrors Again

For far too long, Wolves have faced relegation from the Premier League of Crookedness and Cunning. But NOT ANY MORE! says top reporter, Lurker P. Wolf.

Recent opinion polls among the brute beasts of Frettnin Forest awarded wolves a shaming 3 out of 10 for Slipperiness and Slybootery and a mere 2 for Terror! Asked the question, "Who put the shiver in the The Shivery Sea?" 99% of our readers checked the *Captain Froshus* box.

Well now, thanks to Little Wolf, his bothersome brother, Smellybreff, and their courageous chums Yeller Wolf, Normus Bear, and Stubby Crow, all that has changed. Lupines are back on top of the Terror polls, and the mighty pirate Captain Froshus has been exposed as none other than the foxy Master of Disguises — Mister Twister.

Read how Twister and his huge harsh crew were captured and put to flight by just five ferocious fluffballs.

Read how Little Wolf's exploits outshone those of his great ancestor Blackfur the Backbiter.

Read how he earned the even more fearsome name of:

BLACKFUR THE BOTTOMBITER!

Also by Ian Whybrow
and illustrated by Tony Ross

Little Wolf's Book of Badness

Little Wolf's Diary of Daring Deeds

Little Wolf's Haunted Hall for Small Horrors

Little Wolf, Forest Detective

Dear Little Wolf

Little Wolf's Handy Book of Poems

Little Wolf, Pack Leader